Malay Canoe

Malay Canoe

Clive Dalton, PSEU

Frederick S. Clarke

illustrated by David Knight

Coward-McCann, Inc. NEW YORK

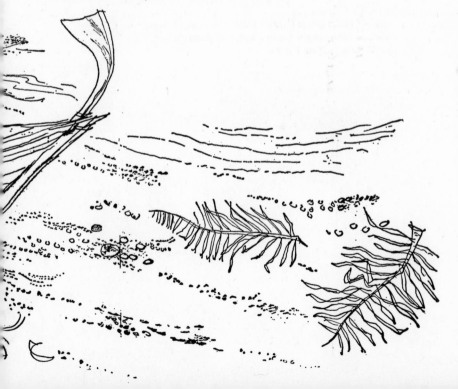

to ANNE *who likes little boys*

The name Kitchie comes from the Malay word *kechil* meaning little, and is often used by the Malays as a pet name for children.

Contents

1 *Kitchie makes a friend*

Old Ali looked up, and his wizened brown face creased into a smile as he saw the small figure approaching him.

"Hai, Kitchie!" he called.

"Hai, Venerable One," said Kitchie, and took up his position a few feet away, squatting on his heels in the sand.

Ali went on scraping the already smooth sides of a nearly finished canoe. Old Ali was one of the finest canoe makers in all Malaya, and Kitchie liked nothing better than to watch him at work.

Some day Kitchie intended to make his own canoe. His bigger brothers and some of his friends already had canoes of their own, and in them they sailed out to meet the big liners coming into the harbor from the west. Like herring about a whale the small canoes would cluster around the big ships, and to the shrill cries of "Penny I dive! Penny I dive!" their occupants dived into the water after the coins that were thrown by the people on the ships.

It was a thrilling and profitable pastime. Some of the boys returned from these adventures with a good sum of money—all sorts of coins from most of the countries of Europe; and the Chinese shopkeepers in the village changed them for the cents in use on the island, at a more than reasonable profit to themselves.

But Kitchie was not anxious about the money. A canoe meant much more than that. A canoe to a Malay boy of the islands was almost the first necessity of life. It meant adventure: the chance to sail out alone upon the glistening seas and to explore the many tiny green islands scattered around.

"You like to watch while I make the canoe," said Ali, who knew very well what was in the boy's mind. "It takes a long time to make a canoe, Little One," he said gently. "And it takes many years to learn to make one well."

The old man raised his eyes to where many of his little craft bobbed gently on the waters beside the *kampong* —the cluster of wooden, palm-thatched huts, built on poles over the sea, that was the Malay village. The canoes were shapely, graceful things which almost came to life when handled with the skill of these brown men of the sea.

"Some day," Kitchie said, "I will make one, and I will sail it out to the small islands."

Old Ali wagged his head sorrowfully. He would have liked to help, but how could he! He couldn't afford to make canoes for nothing, any more than Kitchie's father could afford to buy one; and he knew, far better than his small friend, just how far away was this lovely dream.

Quite suddenly Kitchie was aware that they were no longer alone. He looked up and saw a boy of about his own age standing a few feet away—a boy whose skin, though tanned by the sun, was much fairer than Kitchie's, and who wore, instead of the checked sarong and loose smock of the Malays, the khaki shorts and white shirt of the Europeans.

A white boy!

Ali glanced up, too, and went on with his work.

It wasn't usual for white boys to penetrate into the kampongs of the Malays.

For a while the two boys watched in silence. The brown boy stole a furtive and slightly suspicious glance at the intruder. The white boy ventured an uncertain grin. His face was frank and open and spotted with freckles.

Kitchie shifted uneasily. He was unused to white boys; they were inhabitants of another world and their ways were haughty. There hadn't been many of them on the island of Palau Mati, and of the few there had been, none had taken any notice of the Malays.

But it was clear that this one was different. There was certainly no haughtiness about him. He was frankly curious and even friendly. His eyes traveled from the canoe to old Ali's wrinkled brown face and back again to the canoe.

"Plenty good canoe," he said, in that sort of English which he knew a Malay would be likely to understand. "I'd like one like that!"

To Kitchie, who also understood the pidgin English, which was the usual language used between the Europeans, Malays, and Chinese, the remark was startling. What was this? A white boy with the same dreams as himself! Such a thing was unheard of. What would a white boy want with a canoe?

The old man was grinning slightly. These white people! They could never handle canoes, not the delicate craft of his making, anyway. Canoes required poise and skill in the handling. It was a thing a man must be born to.

An impulse that was partly mischievous made him ask, "You sail canoe?"

"I'll try," answered the boy, with unhesitating confidence.

"All right, you try!"

The three got to their feet; the white boy full of eager excitement; the brown boy full of wonderment and a little uncertain; and old Ali chuckling to himself in anticipation of the fun that was to be.

By the edge of the water was a canoe. Ali pushed it half into the water, and without waiting for anything further, the English boy jumped in and wriggled into a sitting position. Ali gave a shove and the small craft glided smoothly into the water. The boy reached for a paddle that lay in the bottom of the canoe. The two watchers noticed with approval that he held it correctly, his right hand over the top of the handle, his left low down near the blade. He dug the paddle deep into the water, and an unseen hand seemed to pluck at it from somewhere underneath. The canoe lurched wildly. The boy righted himself, but the damage was done. The canoe was behaving like a bucking horse. The boy's arms waved frantically, and then he was in the water. He came up, shook the water from his hair and swam to the shore, where he stood panting and grinning a little sheepishly.

The Malays chuckled with delight. The old man turned to Kitchie.

"Show him!" he said in Malay.

It was Kitchie's turn, and he needed no second bidding. He ran into the water, regardless of his clothes, and righted the overturned canoe. In a second he was aboard. He took up his position, not sitting as the white boy had done, but kneeling with his knees pressed close together and squatting back on his heels. The paddle swept into the water and the canoe leaped forward like a live thing.

"See!" said the old man.

The English boy stood dripping water, but admiration shone in his eyes.

"He's good!" he said.

Kitchie swerved the canoe around and brought it crunching onto the beach. He might be excused for looking a little pleased with himself.

He clambered out and the two boys regarded each other with a new interest. The doubt and suspicion had gone, the shy interest remained and there was a new warmth in the eyes of both.

"What's your name?" asked the English boy.

"My name is Abdul Aziz bin Zainalabidin."

The other blinked in dismay.

"But that's not what he"—indicating Ali—"called you," he protested.

"I call him Kitchie," Ali said. "Little One. Plenty Malay children called Kitchie."

"Then I'll call him Kitchie, too," said the other with a sigh of relief. "My name's Richard," he added, to complete the introduction.

So the friendship began.

In the days that followed, the two boys met again and soon there seemed nothing unusual in the friendship of the Malay boy with an English boy. The halting pidgin English gradually expanded. Kitchie began to learn the language of his new friend, and it wasn't long before Richard began to learn a few words of Malay.

Together they explored the beaches and the rocks and the tall green forests that grew in such tangled confusion on the island.

Then came a day when Kitchie took his new friend into the kampong. They walked along narrow planks stretched from house to house. It was difficult at first, for the planks sagged alarmingly, and once or twice Richard nearly overbalanced and had to wave his arms like a tightrope walker to save himself from falling into the sea. But it was all tremendously exciting.

Boats were tied up under the houses; slender canoes like those in which he had his earlier adventure, and bigger sampans with thatched roofs over the center seats. In one of these Richard had traveled with his parents on a shopping expedition to the mainland.

Everywhere he was regarded with a friendly curiosity, and a few spoke to him in the pidgin English common to the island.

Kitchie and Richard went right through the village to the farthermost huts, where they could see out across the sea to the big ships coming into harbor. Then they came back across the swaying planks, passing from house to house until they reached the beach.

A Javanese was approaching. He wore a big hat, and from a stick slung across his shoulders were suspended what looked like two cupboards. He let his burden down with a grunt, and almost immediately half a dozen children were around him.

"Come," said Kitchie. "We eat."

This was a sort of traveling café. The man squatted in front of his two cupboards and began to open doors and little drawers. Before long a bewildering assortment of Malayan delicacies was spread out before them.

There was a good deal of haggling before any purchase was completed. Kitchie came over to his friend holding out something wrapped in a piece of plantain leaf. Richard took it doubtfully, nibbled at it, and found it to be sweeter than anything he had ever tasted.

"Good!" he said, beaming.

They munched contentedly for a while in silence. The velvety brown eyes of the Malay boy met those of his new friend and they smiled.

The friendship was sealed.

2 Wanted—a canoe

A little apart from the sprawling Malay kampong was another smaller collection of huts built on dry land, with some half-dozen stores skirting the road. It was here that the small Chinese group lived: a handful of tradesmen who served both Malays and Europeans with most of the necessities and some of the little luxuries of life on the island.

Typical of these was the plump Ah Chee who kept a fruit store which he managed with the assistance of his son, Ah Wong. Wong was small and plump and bland. His eyes were narrow and black, and his hair was cropped close. He faced life with a perpetual smile.

Kitchie came to Ah Chee's store, bringing his friend to buy durian. A durian is a strange fruit. It has a very strong and unpleasant smell but Malays like it. Richard, who still had a lot to learn about the ways of the brown people, didn't know this. He hadn't even seen a durian.

The purchase took time.

It began amicably enough, but as soon as the question of price was reached an argument began, which grew so fierce and so noisy it seemed it could only end in blows.

Wong smiled blandly but stood his ground; Kitchie was scornful and angry. Richard watched the whole business with growing astonishment. In his experience one entered a store, stated one's wants, asked the price, and that was that. If the price was too much, one said "No thanks!" and walked out. If the price was satisfactory one paid, and the transaction was complete. But here, it seemed, things were different. His knowledge of Malay wasn't sufficient to enable him to follow the argument, but it was quite clear that it had already gone far

beyond the original question of the price of fruit. It sounded as if Wong and Kitchie were shouting insults at each other.

At last Kitchie, with a final hoot of disgust, turned on his heel and began to walk off, leaving Richard gazing after him in bewilderment. But Kitchie didn't get far. Wong called to him and with a smile more engaging than usual, held out the fruit temptingly.

Kitchie stopped dead and barked a question. For a moment Richard thought the argument was going to break out all over again, but this time the deal was closed, apparently to the entire satisfaction of both parties, and Kitchie walked away with his prize.

It was an odd-looking fruit: about the shape of a football and not a great deal smaller. It was green and covered with a thick, tough rind, which in turn was covered with spikes. Richard had already eyed the thing with misgivings.

Kitchie led the way down toward the beach and past the kampong until they came to a little secluded cove. They sat down and Kitchie began the job of opening up the fruit, which was a matter for an expert. He had brought a strong knife with him for the purpose, and he inserted it into a kind of seam in the rind. His head was bent over his work and Richard couldn't see quite what happened after that. All he knew was that suddenly an overpowering smell was upon him. It was like nothing he'd ever smelled before, and he could only clap his fingers to his nose and back away.

Kitchie looked up and frowned.

"Plenty good," he declared, and plucked out a piece of pulpy white fruit which he held out to his friend. Richard recoiled, shaking his head. Kitchie stared, shrugged, and popped the fruit into his own mouth.

There were other occasions when Kitchie tried to persuade Richard to sample the delights of this wonder-fruit, but Richard never gave in. The smell was too much.

The little cove where they were now sitting was a place they had made their own. It was a sheltered little spot with rocks all around, and a fringe of trees behind the beach. Almost every afternoon they were there, sometimes sitting on the beach and talking, sometimes swimming in the clear water.

In the morning Richard went to school on another island where there were other European children; but there was no school in the afternoon, and he was free to join Kitchie at the cove.

Kitchie was curious about school and its object, and about England. Richard told him what he could: England was a gray, dull sort of a place where the sun shone only on occasion and the land was covered with buildings. School was a fiendish invention of adults to keep children out of trouble.

"Of course, you learn to read and write—and other things," Richard added, a little reluctantly.

By this time they had learned a good deal of each

other's language and could talk quite freely both in English and Malay. In other ways, too, they had learned a lot from each other.

Richard, already a fairly good swimmer, could now dive right to the bottom, keeping his eyes open under the water. He had also learned how to dive for pennies, which was a lot more difficult than it looked, because coins don't fall through water in a straight line but are apt to zigzag wildly on their downward course. The secret was to dive well below the coin, at an angle, coming up underneath it and keeping a sharp eye on its varying direction. The two boys had practiced this in the cove—one throwing the coin and the other diving after it—until both had become expert.

Another odd accomplishment Richard had learned from Kitchie was the art of picking up small objects with his toes, a thing at which all Malays are expert.

In return Richard told Kitchie a great many things about his own country, along with a smattering of such history and geography as he had found interesting enough to remember. The recital of these things among the boys of Kitchie's race soon began to gain Kitchie a reputation for much uncommon knowledge.

So the friendship progressed through the long sunny days, and there remained only the question of the canoe.

If only they could have a canoe of their own, their happiness would be complete.

"Do you think we could make one?" Richard suggested hopefully.

Kitchie shook his head sadly. He knew too much to think that a canoe could be made as easily as that. Hadn't he watched old Ali, who was acknowledged to be the best canoe maker for miles around? Even Ali took a long, long time to make a canoe, with all his skill and knowledge and the tools of his trade right at hand.

"You cut a tree," Richard said, "and you shape it and hollow it out."

"You must know the right tree," said Kitchie. "And you must have the tools. And even then it takes many moons. Also, when it is finished, if it floats at all, it may float on one side, or turn right over and float upside down, so that everyone laughs and the canoe is no good."

Richard thought for a while.

"I suppose," he ventured, "it takes an awful lot of money to buy one?"

"Even my father cannot afford one," Kitchie said, as though that disposed of the matter forever.

Richard frowned into space. There must be a way. If you wanted a thing badly enough and made up your mind about it and never let anything put you off, there was always a way, somehow, some day.

But how?

He glowered across the gleaming waters at a passing junk, but no ideas came. There was no easy answer to this question. He wasn't sure there was an answer.

He supposed that his father could afford to buy a canoe, but he knew it was useless to hope for that. Richard's father had raised no objection to his playing with native boys, but he would certainly not buy them a canoe for a plaything.

Maybe if he saved and saved . . .

No, that was no good. It took months and months to save enough to buy a box of handkerchiefs for his mother's birthday.

It called for some very special effort, or some particular act of fortune. Sometimes these very special things did happen—perhaps an idea, or a stroke of luck, or a very great effort. Just now he couldn't imagine what it could be, or how it could possibly be done; but the important thing was to hold fast to the idea, to make up your mind really hard about it, and to do anything— anything at all—that might be necessary when the very special occasion arrived.

The Malay boy, who never had any hope of owning a canoe, had already dismissed the idea as out of reach. It was obviously impossible for him to have a canoe until he was a grown man—and he could count himself lucky if he got one then—so what was the use of fretting about it? It couldn't be done, and the sensible thing was to for- get about it and enjoy the things one had: the sun, the sea, the fruits of the earth.

"Come!" he said. "Let us swim."

He loosened his checked sarong and let it fall about his feet. It took Richard no longer to whisk off his shorts and shirt, and in a moment the two of them were splash- ing happily in the clear, warm water.

For the moment all else was forgotten.

3   A fine effort

"There's only one thing to do," Richard said, with an air of absolute finality. "If we want a canoe, we'll have to make one ourselves."

Kitchie regarded him with wide-eyed wonder. There were times when he thought all English people were mad, but he had always thought Richard was an exception.

"Make canoe!" he gasped.

Richard nodded, and there was a look of determination on his young face.

"How do you think we'll ever get one otherwise?" he wanted to know. "We can't buy one, and nobody is going to give us one."

Kitchie made a wry face. There was no denying the truth of Richard's words; but to make a canoe was no easy task. He was sure that Richard had no idea of the size of the job he was suggesting, whereas Kitchie knew very well just what it meant. For years he had watched old Ali at his work, and he knew that even with all the tools and materials at hand, it called for a great deal of skill and experience to make even a moderate sort of canoe. How could they, with none of these things, hope to produce anything that would even float on the water? Did Richard imagine they could do the job with a penknife, like making a model yacht?

"No can do!" Kitchie said, glumly shaking his head.

Richard glared. Now he was annoyed with Kitchie for giving up so readily.

"We can try," he protested. "However it turns out, we won't be any worse off."

"Much time, much work," said Kitchie, who like all Malays had no particular liking for work. "And at the end—nothing!"

Richard almost snorted his disgust.

"Oh, all right," he growled. "If you won't help, I'll try it myself."

Kitchie shrugged helplessly. He knew it was useless to argue once Richard had made up his mind. For his part, Kitchie would have been only too pleased to share his friend's enthusiasm if he had thought there was any chance of the plan's succeeding; but he was sure it wouldn't. Richard just didn't realize the tremendous difficulty of the job he was so optimistically suggesting.

"Well," Richard said resignedly, "if you won't help, at least you can give me some ideas. You spend enough time watching Ali."

This was a different matter. At least Kitchie did know something about making canoes, and he was willing enough to talk about it. So, almost without being aware of it, Kitchie found himself getting interested in the idea of making a canoe for themselves. Besides, he liked airing his greater knowledge, and soon he was talking and explaining with as much eagerness as Richard had shown.

Kitchie knew two ways. The first was to build the canoe, starting with the keel and then making a framework of ribs onto which the frame was fastened bit by bit. This was certainly the better way for the experienced craftsman, but it called for a lot of skill and experience which neither of them possessed.

The other way was simpler, and was used by the older men in the kampong. It consisted simply of cutting the canoe out of solid wood. This meant a lot of really hard work, but it didn't require so much knowledge of boatbuilding, and was really the best one for the two boys to attempt. In fact it was the only one they could hope to try.

"We'll do it that way," Richard said with an assurance that made Kitchie feel sorry for him. Did he really think it was going to be as simple as that?

"Need plenty big tree," said Kitchie practically.

"Well," Richard said, with a glance at the jungle towering behind them, "there's no shortage of trees!"

"Take long, long time."

"I know it will, but it doesn't matter how long it takes."

Kitchie sighed. He knew it was useless to try to convince his friend that the job was almost impossible and practically sure to fail. The only way to convince him was to let him try and find out for himself.

"First thing to do," said Richard, now fairly bubbling over in his enthusiasm, "is to find the right tree. It'll have to be pretty thick, because it must be wide enough to sit in. Then we'll have to cut it down and cut off a length of about six to eight feet. That'll be the hardest part of the job. Once that's done . . ."

There followed a great deal of argument and planning, Richard eagerly confident, Kitchie cautious, trying to curb the other's easy optimism.

They would need tools. Richard could probably get a chopper from the Chinese houseboy at home. Kitchie could get a *parang*, a short broad-bladed implement used by the Malays both as a weapon and for clearing jungle. This turned out to be specially useful, for all the bigger trees were deep in the jungle and the boys could only reach them by hacking their way through the undergrowth. The parang was ideal for the job.

So the plans progressed.

It didn't take them long to find what they thought was a suitable tree, and work started immediately.

They marked a line on the trunk, about two feet from the ground, and were about to start when Kitchie held up his hand.

"Wait!" he said, and to Richard's astonishment began

to speak to the tree in formal Malay which was beyond Richard's understanding.

"What on earth was all that for?" Richard asked when Kitchie had finished his solemn little speech.

Gravely Kitchie explained. The Malays believe that every tree is inhabited by its own particular spirit, and no Malay will cut down a tree before making his apologies to the tree spirit and politely requesting it to seek another home; otherwise there is sure to be trouble.

The little ceremony over, the two boys began their task. Stationing themselves one on either side they began to chop along the line they had marked. The outer bark was soon removed, but after that the wood was harder and neither Richard's chopper nor Kitchie's parang made very deep impressions.

They found that it was best to make first a downward cut and then an upward cut so that little wedges were chipped out, making a V-shaped cut. Of course, it would have been much quicker and easier to have used a tree saw, but that was something neither of them could get.

Soon their arms were aching and they were perspiring freely. It just wasn't possible to keep on under the hot sun without a break. They put down their tools, walked to the empty beach and plunged into the sea. The water was warm, but it refreshed them and after a time they went back to their task with renewed energy.

So it went on, but it dismayed them to see what little

impression they had made. It was certainly going to take a long time; several days at the very least.

At the end of three days they were less than halfway through the tree trunk, and even Richard was beginning to get a little discouraged. It was almost frightening to think that this was only the beginning of the job. When they had felled the tree, they had to cut right through it again to get the necessary length, then level it off, shape it, and hollow it out. It would take months! Kitchie nobly resisted the temptation to say "I told you so!" because he was really sorry for Richard, who had started out with such optimism and energy and was now beginning to flag visibly.

Maybe it was lucky that there was an interruption at this point in the form of a compulsory visit to some neighbors. These things didn't occur very often, but when they did, Richard hated them because they upset his normal carefree existence and forced upon him such unpleasant trappings as shoes and a tie, and confined him within the four walls of a room.

Kitchie, for his part, was only too glad of a rest from the arduous work which Richard's friendship had thrust upon him, and he spent the day happily enough in his own particular way in the kampong.

After that, Richard was ready to resume the attack on the tree with new zest, and the next two days saw some real progress.

They had gone around the tree from all sides and the part they had been cutting had taken on the shape of an hourglass. It was possible now, by reaching up high and pushing hard, to make the top part of the tree sway a little. It began to look as though they really might succeed in getting it down.

This presented a new problem. The tree was large and heavy, and when it fell it would fall with a great crash. They must make sure that the tree came down in the direction they wished, toward the sea. And they must be sure that there was no danger of either of them being in the way when it crashed.

After much thought and discussion they decided that the way to do this was to get a rope and tie it to the

upper part of the tree. As the cutting proceeded they would pull on the rope from time to time until they felt it beginning to give, and then at the exact moment, they would give a final pull and both jump clear.

Kitchie got the rope. Just how he managed it Richard never found out, but he was satisfied that they had it. Very gingerly, watched anxiously by his friend, Kitchie ventured up the tree to a height of about ten feet and tied the rope around the trunk. The tree swayed a little, and Richard sighed with relief as Kitchie jumped safely to the ground.

Cautiously they risked a slight pull on the rope. Nothing happened. The tree was as solid as though no cut had been made on it. They pulled harder, and harder still, until they were pulling with every ounce of their combined strength. The topmost branches swayed a little, as though stirred by a puff of wind, nothing more. Clearly, there was still a great deal more hacking to be done.

So they went back to their cutting, pausing now and then to pull on the rope as they had planned, but there was no noticeable difference. The ground was littered with chips from the tree, their arms ached, and they had to take longer and longer rests. Kitchie grumbled a good deal and would have given up altogether, but Richard urged him on, and set the example with his own determined effort.

For two more days they worked, and now it looked as though the slender, remaining piece couldn't possibly hold the weight of the tree.

Once more they pulled on the rope.

There was a sudden sharp crack, like a pistol shot. Both boys dropped the rope and ran in opposite directions, their hearts beating fast.

The tree still stood.

They looked up at it and then looked at each other, hardly able to believe their own eyes. Then cautiously they began to walk toward it.

There was another sharp crack that halted them in their tracks. It was followed by a rending, splintering sort of sound. The great tree swayed, leaned forward uncertainly, and then came hurtling down with a great crashing of branches.

Somewhere in the jungle a bird gave a terrifying screech.

The two boys stood still, gazing in awe at the dreadful thing they had done, and in that moment both of them wished they had never thought of making a canoe.

Another two days passed before they had the heart to resume their work. True, they had accomplished the hardest part of their task, but they felt as though they had committed a crime. The sight of that great tree falling like a stricken thing had filled them both with a strange remorse, and if it had been in their power to restore it they would have done so.

But the thing was done, and they might as well carry on with their plan.

So began the next part of the job: to trim a log to the required length and shape.

It was very much the same business over again, but the work was made a little easier by the fact that the tree now lay flat on the ground. This not only made it more accessible, but meant they could sit down to their work.

In a week they had the log cut to size and had started to taper off both ends, which had already been done in part by the method of cutting.

It was still a long and wearisome task, but they were encouraged by what they had already accomplished.

Then they began to turn their attention to hollowing the log out. This was another big problem, and they decided that it might be well to start on the hollowing-out process before they had finished shaping the outside. The two jobs could be worked in together, and would at least provide a little variety.

In the course of shaping the hull they had already flattened off the top of the log a little, and now they began to dig into it with chopper and parang. After an hour's work they looked at the results with dismay. This was going to be the longest job of all. It would take weeks.

Richard stared at the log, frowning thoughtfully. There must be an easier way! Hadn't he read about it somewhere?

It came to him suddenly. The thing could be burned out! With a return of some of his old enthusiasm, he explained the idea to Kitchie, who received the suggestion with a readiness he had never shown for any of Richard's former schemes. Anything that saved work was welcome!

The next day Richard managed to obtain some matches and the scheme was tried. They collected dried leaves and some of the chips from the tree and made a little mound in the center of the log. Everything was very dry and caught fire quickly, but the fire soon died down without even scorching the log. They added more chips, but the tree still had sap in it and wouldn't catch fire.

Most of that afternoon was spent in fire lighting, but by sunset they had only scorched the surface of the log. However, their efforts, aided by the heat of the tropic sun, had gone a long way toward drying out the log, and when they came back the next afternoon it was, although they didn't realize it, much more likely to burn.

Once again they lighted little piles of leaves and chips, and continued to heap on more chips as the fire burned low. After a time little flickers of flame began to run along the log. The boys fed them with more chips and slowly, to the accompaniment of a hissing of the sap, the fire began to take hold.

They stood back and watched it with satisfaction. Gradually the fire gained until the log began to blaze fiercely.

It was Kitchie who asked the vital question.

"How does it know when to stop burning?"

Richard gave a yell of dismay. Of course! The fire wasn't just burning out the inside; it was going to destroy the whole log. What an idiot he had been not to think of that before!

"We'll have to roll it into the sea!" he shouted.

But it was too late. The flames now enveloped the log and it was burning so fiercely that it forced them back. All their work was crumbling before their eyes and there was nothing they could do to save it.

Richard made a desperate effort to beat out the flames with a branch, but it was hopeless. He couldn't get near enough to do any good.

Kitchie gave a sudden cry of alarm.

"The jungle!"

Richard stifled a yell. The fire had reached beyond the log and little spurts of flame shot along the dry undergrowth.

The two boys stood as though rooted to the spot.

There was an ominous crackling and the flames rose rapidly. Birds flew screeching into the air. Suddenly a multicolored snake slithered past them, making for the sea.

For one horrified second they stood watching, and then fled to the beach.

Behind them the jungle was a great mass of flame, which looked as though it might sweep for miles, destroying everything in its path.

It was appalling to think that they had done this.

Shouts from the kampong told them that the fire had now been seen by the Malays.

"It will be all right," Kitchie said. "These things happen often. They know what to do."

"But they can't put that out!" Richard yelled.

"Light more fire, other side," said Kitchie.

It wasn't quite clear to Richard just how this was done. He and Kitchie ran along the beach and mingled with a crowd of excited spectators. There was a lot of shouting and commotion, as a gang of Malays ran around to the other side of the fire. For a time the fire seemed to get fiercer than ever. Then, after what seemed ages to the two boys, it began to die down until there was only a great area of smoldering, blackened earth.

"No harm done," said Kitchie. "All soon grow again."

"Well, thank goodness for that," Richard said with a heartfelt sigh of relief. Then he gave a wry grin. "But," he added, "I don't think we'll have another try at making a canoe!"

4 An uneasy trio

Richard was on his way home from school. His work was done for the day, and already he was thinking of the afternoon he would spend with Kitchie and the things they would do together.

A sudden movement at the side of the road drew his attention. He looked, and saw something that resembled a very small black lobster.

He knew at once that it was a scorpion. His father had often warned him of them. They were small and fairly harmless-looking things but, in fact, they were very dangerous. If a scorpion was touched, the pincers made a grab and held with a grip of iron, and the tail came over in a flash. On the end of the tail was a point, and behind the point a ball of deadly poison.

All this Richard knew, but it wasn't easy to believe that anything so small could be really dangerous. Why, he had caught bigger crabs!

The scorpion was crawling along in no great hurry, and Richard, on a sudden impulse, placed his exercise book in its path.

His heart beat a little faster as he watched the scorpion crawl onto the book. Should he risk it? It would be something to catch a scorpion alive. Later he could have it preserved and put in a jar, as he had seen them in the house of a friend of his father's.

Gingerly Richard picked up the book. The scorpion began to move toward his hand. Quickly Richard turned the book so that the thing was walking away from him. It came to the edge of the book, found it could go no farther, and turned again. Again Richard switched the book around.

There was a sudden cry, a rush of bare feet, and the book with its deadly burden was knocked from his hand.

Startled, Richard had a momentary glimpse of a small blue-clad figure as it flashed by.

And there was his precious scorpion on the ground and a great stone was thrown upon it, crushing it into a horrible—but harmless—mess.

"Fool!" the newcomer shouted in Malay. "You want to die quick?"

Then Richard recognized the intruder. It was Ah Wong, the little plump Chinese boy from the fruit store, with whom Kitchie had argued about the durian.

"You've killed my scorpion!" Richard shouted.

"Better kill scorpion or scorpion kill you," Wong answered.

"But I wanted to . . ."

Tears of mingled rage and disappointment filled Richard's eyes and he hurled himself upon the astonished Chinese boy, knocking him to the ground. Blind with fury, he raised his fist and would have crashed it into the face of the now thoroughly scared boy, but suddenly a hand descended on him and pulled him away.

"*Richard!*"

At the sound of that voice Richard's heart gave a jump and all the anger went out of him.

His father!

He got up and the frightened Wong clambered to his feet. The man looked at the two boys, and from them to the book and the crushed remains of the scorpion.

"Just what is all this?" he asked, in an ominously even voice.

The two boys looked at each other. Neither spoke.

"Well?"

Haltingly Richard began his explanation. Halfway through, Wong joined in helpfully. The man listened in silence. When Richard had finished, the man turned to Wong.

"I must thank you," he said in Malay. "You may have saved my son's life. He behaved like a fool." He turned to Richard. "And after this boy had saved you from a very serious injury, and perhaps death, you turned on him . . ."

Richard's face was red.

"I'm sorry, Father," he said.

"Hadn't you better shake hands?"

Uncertainly, Richard looked at Wong, who unexpectedly smiled. Richard's face was sheepish as he held out his hand. The Chinese boy took it rather awkwardly and gave a funny little bow.

"Thank you," Richard said. "I'm sorry I hit you."

The Chinese boy smiled suddenly. It was a wide, friendly sort of smile that seemed to light up his plump yellow face. His eyes went down to the crushed mess that had been the scorpion.

"Plenty bad!" he said. "Please don't touch again."

Richard lowered his eyes. By now he was feeling thoroughly ashamed of himself, and wished there was some way to make amends.

"I go now," said Wong and he would have moved

away, but Richard impulsively put out a hand to stop him.

"No, don't go. I'd like . . ." He was suddenly red in the face again. "I really am sorry, I was a fool . . . Would you . . . er . . ." He looked appealingly to his father, who nodded encouragement. "Would you like to come and play with me?"

Again came the wide, illuminating smile.

"Thank you."

They went off together, Richard, Ah Wong, and Mr. Cooper, up the hill toward the spacious house where Richard lived. The two boys were still shy with each other, but already there was a friendly feeling and each knew instinctively that this was the beginning of a friendship.

But to Richard this beginning friendship was already presenting a problem. How was Kitchie going to feel about this? It was nice to have a Malay friend and a Chinese friend. But would the Malay and the Chinese become friends themselves?

Now that he thought about it, he had never seen Malay and Chinese children playing together. Didn't they like each other? This was something he had to find out.

He put the question directly as they walked up toward the house.

"Do you like Malays?"

Ah Wong seemed taken aback and didn't answer for a moment.

"Malays all right," he said, without much conviction.

"Have you any Malay friends?" Richard asked.

"No. Only Chinese friends."

"I have a Malay friend."

Wong nodded blankly. It was obvious that he was neither particularly impressed nor interested, and Richard could see that there was nothing to be gained by pursuing the matter further.

Kitchie's attitude was even more unresponsive on the following day when Richard told him the story of the scorpion and Ah Wong. In no uncertain words the Malay boy expressed the opinion that anyone who attempted to catch a scorpion alive without knowing anything about the things was asking for all he got. And to be rescued from the consequences of one's own foolishness by a mere Chinese was the final ignominy.

"But he's quite a nice guy, really," Richard ventured.

Kitchie's face expressed unutterable scorn. A *nice* Chinese! There was no such thing!

Once again it was clear to Richard that he had reached a deadlock.

Nevertheless, he didn't intend to give up his scheme. It was going to be very, very difficult, but somehow Wong and Kitchie had to be brought together. For the present all he could do was to strengthen his own friendship with Ah Wong while remaining on good terms with Kitchie, and it wasn't easy to manage both these things.

He saw Kitchie almost every day, Ah Wong only occasionally, but whenever he saw Wong, Kitchie always seemed to know and there was a marked coolness in his manner toward Richard for the next couple of days. He couldn't talk about one to the other, and the problem of bringing them together was as insurmountable as the problem of the canoe.

Richard lay awake at night thinking about these things. He was completely alone in this. His friends wouldn't help, and it wasn't the sort of thing to take to his parents.

He dreamed up wild schemes and sadly dismissed them as impossible. It seemed that some outside help was needed, but when could it come? What would it be?

The two problems merged into one in his mind: how to keep both friends, and get a canoe. Solve one and he would solve the other: one master stroke that would accomplish the two things in one, and all would be well. But what?

The days lengthened into weeks and he was no nearer to a solution.

There was no sign of a miraculous intervention.

Richard's usually unshakable optimism began to waver. It was no use. His dreams of the three of them sailing their own canoe across the sunny waters to those enchanting little islands that were tantalizing blobs of green in the shimmering distance would never materialize. He must learn to accept the fact as calmly as Kitchie faced problems, and say with him *Tidapa!* Never mind!

5 Found on the beach

Richard was sitting alone on a large boulder and idly tossing small stones into the sea when Ah Wong came along.

"Hai!" Wong said in greeting.

"Hello!" said Richard, looking up with a start.

Wong stood there, plump and smiling, with a slightly mysterious look on his broad face.

"Come!" he said, turning to lead the way.

"Where?"

"I show you."

"You show me what?"

"You see."

Richard frowned. Although he had been doing nothing in particular, he didn't want to be disturbed unnecessarily. Wong's vagueness annoyed him a little, and, besides, it was Richard who was accustomed to taking the lead. Why should Wong take it upon himself to give the orders?

"What's all this?" Richard demanded. "Where do you want me to go, and what for?"

Wong's smile broadened a little.

Torn between curiosity and annoyance, Richard reluctantly got to his feet.

"Where do you want me to go and why?" he demanded again.

"You see!" said Wong.

It was obvious that the Chinese boy was bubbling with suppressed excitement.

"At least you can give me an idea what it's all about," Richard protested.

Wong shook his head, and catching hold of Richard's hand, began to lead him toward a jungle path that cut across to the other side of the island.

It was evident that whatever Wong's secret was, he had no intention of revealing it until the moment was right. It was equally clear that it was no joke but a matter of real importance. Something of Wong's excitement had already communicated itself to Richard, and when Wong broke into a trot, Richard lost no time in following his example.

The path led them across to a quiet beach at a remote corner of the island seldom used by either Chinese or Malays. It was rocky here and the beach sloped deeply. It was known that sharks were often found in the waters close to the shore.

They came around a corner of rocks, and there was the empty beach. Wong stopped abruptly and flung out his arm in a dramatic gesture.

"See!"

Richard looked and drew a quick breath.

There, lying on its side in the middle of the beach, was a canoe. A fine big canoe.

"Great Scott!" he cried. "Whose is it?"

"Belong to nobody," Wong said. "Come in on tide. Empty. Nobody touch it. Flightened ghosts!"

Richard's head whirled. A fine big canoe washed up by the tide, belonging to nobody, claimed by nobody! Theirs for the taking.

They almost fell down the beach to get to the canoe. As they came closer they could see an ugly gash along the side, evidently where the craft had hit some jagged rock. Already Richard was wondering what could have happened to its owner. Drowned, no doubt. The craft might have drifted for days, even weeks.

They came closer and stood staring at it, wondering. Dare they claim it? Would there be trouble if they took it? It was damaged, of course, but not badly. With Kitchie's help they would be able to patch it up.

Kitchie! Wait till he heard of this! Richard could already imagine his excitement—and this would establish Wong with him. In a sudden flash he saw that the problem of making Kitchie and Wong friendly with each other was going to be miraculously solved.

Wong had indeed done a fine piece of work.

"We must tell Kitchie!" Richard said excitedly. His eyes went back to the canoe. "Do you think we ought to hide it so that no one else can find it?"

Wong shook his head decisively.

"Nobody touch it," he said with absolute conviction.

Richard frowned. It was like a cloud over this sunny morning. Nobody would touch it. Why? Because they were afraid. Afraid of the ghost of a dead man coming up from the sea, perhaps to lay a curse on this boat.

Would Kitchie feel like that about it? There was only one way to find out.

"Come," he said. "Let's go and find Kitchie."

Without further discussion they set off toward the kampong, Richard leading, plump Wong puffing a little as he followed behind. It wasn't hard to find Kitchie. He was with old Ali, the pair of them squatting on their heels and regarding an almost completed canoe with professional interest.

He showed no pleasure at the sight of the other two.

"Hello!" Richard called out. "Hey, Kitchie, come with us. We have something to show you."

Kitchie looked up with an expression of complete in-difference.

"What you show?"

"Come and see."

"No come. I stay here," said Kitchie with absolute finality and returned his attention to the canoe.

"Oh, come on," Richard said impatiently. "This is something special."

"You tell me what."

"No. This is a surprise."

Kitchie shrugged.

"You no say, I no come."

Richard glared, struggling hard to control his annoy-ance. He looked at Wong, who was standing helplessly by, a look of mild concern on his yellow face. Richard grinned suddenly, remembering that he had behaved in exactly the same way an hour ago when Wong had ap-proached him in a similar manner.

"Oh, all right," he said, "if you don't want to see it . . ."

"See what?" Kitchie demanded, curiosity struggling with resentment.

"I'm not going to tell you. If you want to see it, you'll have to come with us."

At this point old Ali broke in with a stream of Malay much too rapid for Richard to follow, at the end of which he showed his red betel-stained teeth in a grin that included all three.

Kitchie got to his feet and stood waiting.

"Good!" Richard said and set off without another word.

So they came once more to the beach.

With the air of a conjuror producing a rather special rabbit out of a hat, Richard flung out his arm.

"Look!"

Kitchie looked. His eyes opened wide. Wonder, delight and dismay chased each other across his face.

"Wong find it," said Wong proudly.

"Isn't she a beauty?" Richard said.

But Kitchie wasn't to be won over so easily.

"Who belong?" he demanded.

"Came in on the tide."

"Belong dead man, maybe. We see ghost."

"Oh, rot!" Richard said in exasperation.

Kitchie glowered at the damaged hull. With the air of an expert he ran his hand along the splintered wood and made a wry face.

"We can fix that," Richard said reassuringly.

"Water come in. It sink," retorted Kitchie with awful finality.

"But we can fix it."

"No easy fix it."

"Oh, all right," Richard exploded, goaded beyond endurance. "If you don't want a share in it, you needn't bother. Wong and I will have her ourselves."

Wong's woebegone expression immediately brightened, and Kitchie looked upset.

"No good come of this," he growled, but there was no longer the same conviction in his voice.

It was surprising how all their forebodings disappeared as they began to plan the repair of the canoe.

It was obviously no easy matter. An expert could probably have made her seaworthy in a few hours, but it was another matter for the boys to undertake such a job, especially with neither experience nor tools and only such materials as were at hand.

The first question was whether to enlist the aid of the expert, Ali. Reluctantly they decided that they mustn't, friend though he was. Nobody must know of this. Not even their parents. The whole thing must be kept a secret lest their prize be taken from them.

Later, of course, it would have to be revealed, but not until they had made at least one adventurous voyage.

So they returned to their homes, hugging their precious secret, planning how to tackle the work and dreaming of the day when they would first sail their own canoe.

Then came the real business of the repairs.

The next afternoon they met on the beach and got down to the job in earnest.

The first thing to do was to obtain the materials. They scouted around for wood, of which there was plenty on the beach, until they found what they thought was the right size.

Then the problems began. The wood was flat, whereas the hull of the canoe was generously curved, and it was quite obvious that they couldn't repair a curved surface with a flat patch.

But this problem, surprisingly, almost solved itself.

It was Wong who discovered, with a whoop of triumph, the remains of a broken barrel. Here was wood already curved to something approximating the shape of the canoe.

They tried several pieces, and at last found one that lay reasonably close along the hull. Not exactly. It wasn't as snug and tight as something made to measure, but was still a good fit, and showed only a fraction of space between it and the hull. This space was so slight that it was possible to press upon the middle of the patch until it touched the hull.

But how were they to keep this pressure on the middle?

There followed a good deal of head scratching. Eventually they put the wood on the ground and lugged a boulder over and placed it on the wood, hoping that the weight of the boulder would flatten the wood to just the required shape.

It took some time, but they got the patch so that it fitted nicely.

The next thing was to fasten it in position.

"Screws," Richard said with authority. "They're better than nails."

He had learned this piece of wisdom from his father, who was something of a handyman.

Kitchie remembered that there was some kind of

gummy substance which he had seen old Ali use in the making of canoes. You warmed it and smeared it on, and when it was cold it set hard and was completely waterproof. He could probably get some of this without arousing any suspicion.

So their preparations went ahead.

The next day they met again at the same place. Richard had brought a box of screws, a gimlet and a small screwdriver. Kitchie arrived with half a coconut shell containing the messy-looking substance which was to seal the joint.

Richard took charge of the proceedings, Kitchie helped, and Wong stood by with an expression of vague encouragement on his broad face.

At last, after a good deal of work and a lot of argument, the patch was fixed, and with mixed feelings they stood back to survey their handiwork.

The job looked good; but it had to be tested.

They slid the canoe down the beach and into the water. They knew she would float, but the question now was—would she leak? The water didn't yet reach the joint. She needed weight before the test was complete.

Kitchie clambered in and his weight brought the patch to the level of the water. Richard followed. The canoe rocked and settled and now the water was over the lower part of the patch.

No water seeped through.

They helped Wong aboard and the canoe was well

down. Three pairs of eyes fastened anxiously on the patch.

They sat in silence for several seconds, long anxious seconds, hardly daring to look. The water lapped gently against the hull, but still none came through.

Eyes went from one face to another and back to the patch.

It still held!

They could hardly believe it themselves. But it was true. They had done it. The canoe was sound!

6 Shipwreck

Two days later they set out.

Richard had spent the greater part of those two days making a canoe paddle. The finished result would hardly have delighted the heart of Ali, but it was adequate.

Kitchie already had one—a prized possession which he had found a long time ago, washed up by the tide, and had since treasured, for he had always known that the time would come when he would need it.

Wong's share in the preparations was to provide food —wasn't he the son of a storekeeper? And now he came laden with fruits: bananas and pomelos and thick, juicy sugar cane.

Their objective was a tiny island about a mile to the southwest, a little green mound rising out of the sea and topped by slender palms; an island out of a tale, a place of promise and unpredictable adventure.

Long and often they had gazed at it and longed to cross the water to land on its beaches and explore its mysteries.

Now at last the dream could be fulfilled.

Not a word had been said to anyone else. The canoe had been carefully hidden in the undergrowth, and although all three of them had been bursting with sup-

pressed excitement, each had managed to keep the precious secret.

Having made sure they weren't seen, they brought the canoe from its hiding place and dragged it down the beach. The provisions were loaded and they shoved off, jumping aboard one by one as the craft slid into the sea. Kitchie sat forward with one paddle, Richard aft with the other, and Wong, the passenger, amidships.

They gave a last look around, then dug the paddles into the water.

They were off.

Their craft handled beautifully, sweeping through the water swift and graceful as a bird. Now and again one or the other would cast an eye toward the patch, but there was no sign of a leak.

Rhythmically and in perfect unison the paddles swept the water, one each side of the boat, and the island was no longer a vague blob but a place of sand and trees and rocks. They could see a projecting rock that had the face of a gargoyle.

But they were lost in the sheer joy of their boat, the feel of her gliding through the sea, the music of water lapping the hull, the rhythm of the paddles.

Now they could see the tops of the palms and the gargoyle's face had changed into a rocky crag.

There was a sudden sharp exclamation from Kitchie, and almost in the same instant Richard realized that his feet were wet.

There was an inch of water in the canoe.

All eyes went instantly to the patch. Water was oozing through and the canoe was beginning to settle lower in the water.

"*Ayo!*" Kitchie exclaimed in dismay, and dug his paddle with a new urgency. Richard did the same, and Wong, cupping his hands, began to bale out the water as fast as he could.

The canoe responded nobly, but the beach was still

some forty yards away, and clearly the race was going to be a desperate one.

The provisions were ruined, but that was of little importance now. The vital matter was to reach the shore.

Despite Wong's frantic efforts, water was still rising in the canoe, and she was settling lower in the water. Before she had cleaved through the sea; now she wallowed like a log and was no longer responding to the paddles.

Suddenly, and without warning, she sank under them.

They splayed out into the sea, dropping their paddles and instinctively striking out for the shore. It was well that they were all good swimmers, and the shore wasn't too far away; but there was still the danger of sharks.

The canoe, without their weight, rose to the surface again and lay there, waterlogged and useless, with the two paddles floating close by.

Swiftly and expertly the three boys swam for the beach. They didn't stop to look back at the canoe. Their one thought was to reach the safety of the beach, for these waters were full of untold dangers.

Fear gave them speed, and a few minutes later they were scrambling up the beach to collapse, exhausted and frightened, in three wet heaps.

The canoe lay drifting idly a few yards out. It wasn't worth the risk of trying to beach her. Maybe the tide would bring her in; maybe it would take her out. It didn't really matter, for the one certain fact was that they would never be able to get back in her.

The gravity of their position was slowly coming home to them. They were stranded, and it might be days, even weeks, before they were found.

They had visions of anxious parents scouring the islands, and the wrath that would follow if and when they were found.

"I suppose," Richard ventured, with a brave attempt at optimism, "this place really is deserted?"

Kitchie shot him a withering look.

"Nobody live here. Nobody come here. They will not think to look here. It will be a long time before we are found—if we are ever found."

Wong sat staring in front of him, his usually cheery face the picture of gloom.

"My father will be very angry," he said, more to himself than to either of the others. "And my mother will be very sad."

Richard, who was more cheerful by nature than the other two, found his mind wandering to memories of books he had read: *Robinson Crusoe, The Swiss Family Robinson, The Coral Island*. This was the very stuff of romance. To be cast away on a desert island was real adventure.

It all came back to him. The first thing to do was to explore your island and find out just how you stood for food and shelter. You lived in a cave or a roughly made shelter of palm leaves and bamboo; you looked for fruit and a means of catching fish, and you gradually built up the necessities of existence until by the time you were rescued you were living in comparative comfort.

These thoughts reminded him that he was hungry.

"Anyway," he said, getting to his feet, "we must have a look around."

Kitchie remained scornful.

"What you expect to find?"

"I dunno! There must be fruit of some sort."

"You find nothing! Except snakes, maybe!"

"Well, it's no use just sitting here," Richard flung back. "That won't do any good at all. At least we've got nothing to lose, and you never know what we might come across. There might even be an old canoe . . ."

He realized that this last remark was a little unfortunate and let it trail off; but the general gist of his argument was unanswerable, and Kitchie gave in with a shrug of the shoulders. Wong was already won over.

It was still early in the day, for they had set out shortly after breakfast and it wasn't yet noon by the sun. There was plenty of time for them to explore this very small island before darkness was upon them.

Kitchie put in a word of caution.

"We go around the beach," he said. "Not safe to go into jungle."

"What do you think is there?"

"No know. But nothing good, that sure!"

Richard was in no mood to be put off by the Malay's pessimism. There was a fascination in the exploration of strange places at any time, but now there was more than that; there was the real need to find out all that they possibly could about this island with as little delay as possible.

Their first fears had gone and they were now curious and even enjoying the adventure a little, but there was still the underlying fear: what if they were never found and never saw their homes again? What if there was nothing to eat or drink?

The beach was a soft yellow strip about twelve yards wide which ended abruptly in a wall of solid green jungle: silent, beautiful, yet somehow ominous.

As they walked along the beach, first one then another cast apprehensive glances toward the jungle. It was as though many unseen eyes were watching them from the undergrowth. On the other side was the sea, glistening in the sun, friendly but empty.

There was nothing else in sight.

The plan was to follow the beach and walk right around the island. It didn't look as though this would lead them to any particularly interesting discovery, but this must be the first move, and it wouldn't take long. After that maybe they would make a tentative venture inland, but they must first see if there was anything in the nature of a path, or at least a point where the jungle was less dense.

They walked in silence for a while. Then Kitchie remarked, "We might walk around this island three times without knowing it!"

But Richard was equal to this. He looked behind him, and there was a trail of disturbed sand where they had walked. The sand before them was flat and undisturbed.

"See," he said. "When we come to the point where we started we'll know—"

He stopped suddenly and stood staring ahead with an expression of utter unbelief on his face. The others followed the direction of his glance and were in turn rooted to the spot.

Some twenty yards ahead of them, at a point which they certainly couldn't have covered, the sand was disturbed exactly like that part immediately behind them.

"Look!"

"There must be someone else here after all."

"I wonder . . ."

They looked from one to another and back to the marks in the sand. Hope, excitement and a vague misgiving struggled within them.

This could mean all sorts of different things. It could mean rescue, or it could spell danger. It depended on just who or what had left that trail in the sand. It wasn't really likely to be an animal and, if human, as it almost certainly was, it was more likely to be friendly than unfriendly. After all, the days of savages and pirates and the like were over.

The only question was, what was anybody doing on this supposedly desert island?

He could hardly be a castaway, for this island, though small and deserted, wasn't by any means remote, and anyone shipwrecked here would have been heard of on one of the larger islands sooner or later. Common sense told the boys that, even though they feared they might never be found. Moreover it didn't look as though there were any food on the island, and nobody could have lived here without having supplies brought to him.

However, all these questions could be answered, and there was only one way to find the answer.

"We'll have to investigate," said Richard.

"We be careful," Wong advised.

"Ho, come on," Richard said. "What do you think it is—a wild man from Borneo or something?"

"Could be orangutang!" Kitchie said.

"Rot," said Richard. "You only find orangutangs in the big jungles on the mainland. And there aren't many left, anyway."

So, cautiously, with fast-beating hearts they advanced.

The tracks seemed to lead from the edge of the water

to the jungle so that whoever or whatever it was that had made the tracks had gone into the jungle. But the tracks weren't clear in the soft sand, and they might well be those of someone coming from the jungle to the sea.

As they drew nearer, Kitchie's experienced eye noticed something else. There was a fairly deep straight groove among the marks, which could only have been made by a boat of some sort being dragged through the sand. The groove made it still harder to see which way the tracks were going.

Clearly the occupant of the island was human.

Their steps faltered and they exchanged glances that expressed their qualms. They peered at the wall of jungle where the marks in the sand ended, but there was no sign of anything there. No boat, no hut, not a movement; just that solid, silent mass of foliage.

"I know," Richard said, in a voice that expressed at once relief and disappointment. "There's been someone here but he's gone."

That was, indeed, the obvious and logical explanation, and neither of the others was inclined to disagree.

But one vital question remained: was he coming back?

It was almost certain that he wasn't. This was, in all probability, the stopping place of some casual voyager who had set out, exactly as they had, made a call at this island, rested awhile and gone his way.

That left them exactly where they were, but at least they could now continue their exploration of the island. It was the only thing left to do.

7 The green jungle

The sun was high overhead now, blazing out of an empty sky, turning the sea to a great sheet of molten silver and making the sand hot under their bare feet.

It must have been close to noon, and they were beginning to feel thirsty and a little hungry. They had no particular worries about the immediate future; their only concern now was to find water.

They were about halfway around the island by this time and there had been no change in the landscape except for those marks in the sand. The rest was the same; the soft yellow strip of beach, the green solidity of the jungle, and the empty expanse of sea. If there was a stream anywhere on this island it must surely run down to the sea, but they had seen no sign of any.

They trudged on, hoping, trying to dispel their uneasiness, trying to conceal from each other the mounting fears as the seriousness of their position came home to them.

Richard, in a forlorn attempt at jauntiness, began to whistle. Withering glances from each of his companions silenced his efforts. He gave a disheartened shrug and trudged on in silence.

Suddenly Kitchie gave a shout and pointed ahead. Following the direction of his outstretched arm, they saw a small cluster of palm trees, like giant feather dusters, leaning out over the beach at such a perilous angle that they seemed to be in danger of falling down.

To Richard it seemed that this was little cause for excitement. They had seen palm trees before.

"What's wonderful about that?" he wanted to know.

Kitchie was unable to resist a superior smile.

"Coconuts!" he said briefly, and waited for the effect.

"Coconuts, well . . ." Richard paused, and suddenly realized the significance. Coconuts contained milk. Not much like milk, really; more like a sort of lemonade, but a good drink to a thirsty boy.

"But . . ." He looked up with undisguised alarm at the great height of the trees. "We'd never get one down."

"I get!" said Kitchie, his triumph now complete.

Richard hid his embarrassment. This was Kitchie's moment. It was certain that neither of the others could hope to get a coconut, but if Kitchie had that remarkable ability to climb this tall slender tree, which had no branches but only that feathery cluster of fronds at the top, then he could save them all from the torment of thirst.

They quickened their pace and, as they drew near, broke into a run. In a matter of moments they were at the foot of the trees, which now looked taller than ever.

Richard gazed up and drew a sharp breath.

"It's very high," he said doubtfully. "Do you really think you can do it?"

Kitchie nodded and grinned. To him this was easy. He had climbed coconut palms that were almost vertical. Some of these leaned over at such an angle that it would be almost possible to walk up them.

He rubbed his palms down his sarong, and quickly linked his fingers around the trunk of the nearest tree and began to climb in a series of little hops.

Richard and Wong watched in awe and admiration.

Kitchie went on and up, swift and sure as a monkey, without a downward glance and without a second's hesitation. He seemed to get smaller and smaller, until at last he was lost in the great plume of foliage which crowned the tree.

A coconut came hurtling down to half-bury itself in the soft sand. Then another and another, until there were half a dozen of them.

Then Kitchie came down, just as he had gone up but not quite so quickly. He stood grinning triumphantly in front of them.

"That," said Richard, with heartfelt admiration, "was terrific!"

Wong beamed his agreement. Nobody else could have done this!

Kitchie's grin grew broader; he was enjoying his moment.

"Now we drink," he said.

The nuts were covered with a thick outer skin of tough fiber. First they had to tear this off, and then break the inner shell with a piece of jagged stone. Again Richard was the novice. Both Kitchie and Wong were able to strip the nuts with comparative ease, but Richard's fumbling fingers grew sore before he had half-completed his task.

The cool, sweet juice of the nut was pleasant and refreshing. They drank their fill, and with more stones broke the shell again so that they could chew on the nuts while they went on their way.

Leaving the cluster of palms, they pushed on. They were more than halfway around the island by now, and still there was no sign of any change in the scenery. Throughout their journey they had been buoyed up by the vague hope that they might come upon something. They hardly knew what—a jungle path, some sort of habitation, a clearing, something that would offer them shelter—but there was nothing, and hope was beginning to fade. The prospect of having to spend a night on the beach was something they didn't want to think about.

They came around a corner of rock—that same rock which from the distance had the face of a gargoyle— and there was their canoe, washed up on the beach, and not far away the two paddles left by the receding tide.

This was the point where they had landed. They had walked around the island, and all they had found was a cluster of palms and some footprints in the sand.

It was some little comfort to find the canoe. Useless as she was, if things came to the worst they felt they might somehow patch her up sufficiently to attempt a perilous journey back.

They ran to the craft and hauled her higher up onto the beach so that the next tide wouldn't take her away. She was heavy with water, and there was a pulpy mess in the bottom which was the fruit Wong had brought. They threw it out onto the sand to dry. There might be something eatable there when it dried out, and they might well be glad of it.

And now . . . ?

They sat down to review their position. They realized more and more clearly that they would have to spend a night here, and although none of them lacked courage, it was an alarming prospect.

"We haven't really explored the place," Richard said, speaking slowly. "We've only been *around* it."

He looked inward toward the jungle, and gulped.

"Not go in there," Wong said in undisguised alarm.

"We can go a little way, just to see," said Richard.

"Why?" Kitchie asked.

"Because," Richard said, with some exasperation, "I don't like spending a night on this beach."

"You want to sleep in *there?*" Kitchie demanded incredulously.

"We might find some sticks or something," Richard assured him.

"What for sticks?"

"Well, in case, in case . . ."

"We got canoe paddles," Kitchie said, reading Richard's unspoken thoughts.

"Well, anyway, I think we should have a look. You don't know what we might come across," Richard said.

"All right," said Kitchie, with a suspicion of a grin, "you go!"

"I will, too," Richard snapped, jumping to his feet.

Gritting his teeth he strode determinedly toward the

jungle. The other two exchanged doubtful glances, but Richard went on, unwavering, without a backward glance, straight up to the forbidding wall of green.

He had come to a place where the growth was a little less dense and a little less high, but even here, as he parted the foliage and stepped inside, it seemed to swallow him up.

It wasn't like stepping into a wood; it was like entering another world, a dim green twilight world. Even the smell was different; a vague, dank odor of decay; the ground under his feet was moist and spongy; he felt he was being watched by countless eyes. He wasn't aware of individual trees or bushes; it was a tangled mass of nameless vegetation that seemed to clutch at him, that would hold him so fast in here that he could never get out.

His heart beat so fast that he could feel it thumping against his ribs, but he pushed forward. The jungle held him back, met above his head shutting out the light, even the air; he could hardly breathe . . .

A sound behind him made him spin around.

There stood Kitchie and Wong, each clutching a canoe paddle, each looking just as frightened as he felt.

"Fool!" Kitchie said savagely. "You come out!"

Richard was trying to hide his relief. He could have sworn that the Malay boy was trembling.

"It doesn't look as if we'd find much in here," he said.

"You come out!" Kitchie repeated and grabbed hold of Richard's arm.

They scrambled out into the sunlight with more haste than dignity. They hadn't penetrated far into the undergrowth, but what little they had seen was enough to satisfy them that there was little chance of getting into the interior, and even less chance of their finding anything even remotely useful if they could.

So they must confine themselves to the more friendly beach.

It was well into the afternoon now and the sun was past its zenith. They must begin to consider seriously the question of bedding down for the night.

It would be cold later, and they must find what shelter they could. Obviously the best place was the sheltered side of the big rock.

They went over and examined it. There was a sort of overhanging ledge and a niche that was almost the beginning of a cave. It was a good place for shelter, and could be made still better by scooping out the sand to form a hollow. There they would not only be sheltered from the weather but hidden from sight; not that there appeared to be any great need to be hidden, but they would feel much safer in case anything might come out from the jungle during the night.

"We'll bring the canoe over," Richard said, "and put it there." He indicated the one spot where they might be slightly exposed. "If we shovel the sand over the canoe, it will make a sort of wall."

His spirits were rising, and he was beginning to enjoy the adventure of it again—the Robinson Crusoe touch.

His enthusiasm was infectious, and soon the three of them were working to make their sleeping place. The canoe was dragged over and put in place. Then they began scooping out sand with cupped hands and pouring it over the canoe. In a short time they had dug themselves a snug little nest which offered them a great deal more comfort and security than the open beach. They knew it would be cold at night, and they had nothing with which to cover themselves; but in here they would at least be protected from wind and rain, and they could lie close together, perhaps even covering their bodies with sand if necessary.

Having made these preparations they could now face the prospect of a night on the island with a certain amount of assurance. But secretly they hoped that there wouldn't be many such nights. And how long could they survive on coconuts? Nobody had the least idea, and nobody was particularly eager to find out.

Not long, surely! Already search parties would be out and sooner or later they must be found. Maybe they could do something to speed their own rescue; contrive some sort of signal—a fire perhaps. It could be done with two sticks, but it wasn't easy. Richard had tried it once without success. But now, with necessity as the spur, no doubt he could make a better attempt.

There would be time for that later, if and when it became necessary. No doubt the search was already spreading out and must sooner or later reach this island.

All of them had, though in varying degrees, a feeling

of guilt about the anxiety of their parents, and each wished that there was some way of letting them know that they were safe. But that was impossible. They knew, too, how angry their parents would be after the first relief of getting them safely home. They realized that what to them was a great adventure would seem, in the eyes of parents, nothing but a foolish prank. But that was a thing that would have to be faced, and any punishment was better than being lost forever on this island.

The sun had dipped down toward the horizon and turned the sea into burnished copper. A spectacular tropical sunset shot the whole sky aflame with incredible color and fantastic shapes, followed by the equally brief tropical twilight; and suddenly it was night and the stars began to show like twinkling lights in the velvet blackness of the sky.

The jungle loomed up black and sinister, and already they were aware of a thousand tiny noises, some real, some imaginary. There was the gentle, rhythmic swish of the waves on the beach that was real and friendly. But those vague rustlings and murmurings that seemed to come from the jungle—how many were real and how many just imagined? Certainly none of them was friendly. Again there was the feeling of many eyes watching from the darkness.

"Better get to bed," Richard said, and his voice sounded strangely hollow.

Neither of the others needed any second bidding; the

sleeping space they had made for themselves was like a little fort, and they could feel much safer in there.

They scrambled in and huddled together, talking to keep up their spirits.

The sand was still warm and they dug their feet into it, piling it up over their legs until they were buried to the waist. The rocks and their barrier of sand hid them from the jungle, and already they felt more secure.

They lay looking up at the stars.

For a while they talked in that mixture of kampong Malay and pidgin English which was their common language. They spoke of the adventure and its possible outcome; of how long they might remain here before they were found; of the possibility of repairing the canoe, and of making signals for searchers to see.

Gradually their voices grew drowsy and their talk trailed away until there was only the sound of their breathing mingled with the soft swish of the waves.

8 The man on the beach

They slept soundly. The dawn failed to wake them, and it wasn't until the morning sun was well into the sky that Ah Wong stirred. He blinked around him in puzzled fashion and rubbed his eyes. Then, as consciousness and memory came awake, he turned to rouse the others.

The first thought was breakfast. There were three coconuts left. They broke them open, drank the milk and chewed the nuts. Richard found himself thinking wistfully of bacon and eggs, and the other two had similar longings: for rice and dried fish and various dishes known only to their own peoples.

But if breakfast left something to be desired, the morning washing made up for it. They shed their clothes and ran into the sea to splash happily in the shallows. There was no need to hurry. They swam about lazily, dived down among the multicolored seaweeds and coral growths that made a subterranean garden of the sea bed, and came out to lie luxuriously in the warming sun.

This was a moment of pure joy and the whole adventure was worth while. There was a feeling of immense satisfaction in having successfully come through a full day and night on the island; for if they could do it once they could do it again, though they hoped they wouldn't have to live for very long on a diet of coconut.

That thought brought them to the immediate need to look for food. They had finished the coconuts and sooner or later they must get more. Or was there any hope of finding anything else? Ah Wong's fruit had dried out, but it was still an unappetizing mess and nobody wanted to try it. What then? Perhaps a second, and more venturesome, exploration of the island—the possibility of contriving some means of catching fish. Or, again, maybe they should arrange some sort of signal to attract any ship that might sail nearby.

These things occupied their minds, but with no great urgency; it was pleasant to lie in the sun and let the mind wander lazily. Time had ceased.

Presently Richard stirred.

"Oh, well," he said, "I suppose we'd better have another look around."

He got up and wriggled into his shorts, leaving the shirt, which was his only other garment, on a rock. Kitchie put on his checked sarong, and Wong his blue Chinese slacks, and again they set off to explore their domain.

As before, they started along the beach, but this time in the opposite direction. In the morning sunlight everything looked friendly—even the jungle seemed a brighter green in the early light. Now and then they looked out to sea, and occasionally there were boats cruising around, but none approached the island. Once, when one was so near that they might have been seen, they waved frantically and shouted, but without success.

"He not see us," Kitchie said. "Plenty more not see us. Nobody come here. We be here plenty long time."

"Rot!" said Richard. "Our parents will be looking for us. They're bound to find us soon."

"Yes, soon!" Wong said with his all-embracing smile.

Kitchie grunted, unconvinced, and they walked on in silence for a while.

Presently they could see the tops of the coconut palms waving gently above the other foliage. They rounded a corner of jutting rocks and then stopped dead in their tracks.

There was a man on the beach.

At first they took him for a Malay, for he was wearing the traditional checked sarong and his bare torso was tanned a golden brown. But he had a beard such as no Malay could have grown, and his hair was the color of bronze.

He stared at them unbelievingly. They stared back in astonishment mingled with relief and a little alarm; for this was a strange and rather wild-looking person, and

there was no knowing how he would react to their presence.

He scratched his head. Then he found his voice.

"What the devil are you doing here?" he demanded, and went on without waiting for a reply. "How long have you been here?"

Richard spoke nervously. It was obviously up to him to do the talking.

"We came in a canoe, but our canoe sank and we can't get back."

The man nodded thoughtfully, still eyeing them suspiciously.

"We spent the night on the beach," Richard said, gaining confidence, and added rather plaintively, "And we've had nothing to eat except coconuts since yesterday."

A faint smile flickered across the stranger's face, but he said nothing.

The three boys had been studying him closely and wondering. Who was this strange person, and how had he got here? And what was he going to do about them? Would he take them back, for surely he must have a boat? Had he been here all the time, concealed somewhere in the interior, or had he just arrived?

Kitchie plucked up his courage and butted into the conversation. It was time, he felt, that they ask some questions.

"Tuan got boat?" he asked.

The man shifted his gaze from Richard to the Malay boy.

"Oh yes, I have a boat," he said.

"Maybe take us back?" Kitchie asked hopefully.

The man pursed his lips thoughtfully.

"I don't know yet. I'll have to think what to do about you."

"But you can't leave us here!" Richard burst out. "You must be going somewhere. Can't you take us with you?"

He was beginning to feel uneasy. It was obvious from the start that this man was a very odd person. Now Richard was wondering just how odd he really was.

Was he a crank or a lunatic? Or was he just playing a game with them? It was all very disturbing.

"You don't *live* here, do you?" Richard ventured.

"Maybe I do," said the man.

Richard's expression reflected his disbelief.

"But yesterday we went all around the island, and there was nothing." Then with sudden recollection he added, "Only some marks in the sand."

"I suppose you expected to find a hut on the beach or something like that? Oh no, young man, nothing so obvious," the stranger said mockingly.

"But you don't live in *there*," said Richard, with a shudder as he glanced toward the jungle.

"You ask too many questions," the man said, glaring at them angrily. "I don't know what the dickens I'm going to do with you."

"We only want to get back!" Richard said, rather forlornly. "Our parents will be worried. . . ."

The man turned his head sharply. "Your parents! They'll be looking for you?"

"Bound to be!"

"Little fools!" he burst out angrily. "What the devil did you have to come here for? Here I was nicely settled in and everything arranged, and you have to come along and spoil the whole thing."

Richard shifted uneasily. What did it all mean? Why couldn't he take them back? And if he wouldn't take them back, then what on earth did he intend to do? It was all a little frightening.

"Maybe," the man said, thinking aloud, "I should just go off and leave you here to wait for somebody to find you. And if they don't find you, that'll be just too bad. But why should I give it all up after the trouble I've been to, just for the sake of three kids? On the other hand if somebody does find you, you'll talk. I can't imagine three of you—boys of your age—being able to keep quiet about a thing like this."

"But what else can you do?" said Richard. "You can't keep us here. They'll be looking for us already, and before long they're bound to come here, and then . . ."

"And then," the man said, again with that slightly ominous smile. "They'll find nothing. Oh, I can hide you. You were here for a whole day without knowing there was anything else alive in the place, weren't you? But that's beside the point. The point is, I don't want you here. I don't want anyone here. This is *my* island, and I intend to keep it to myself."

He stared at them, and his eyes seemed to see right through them. They fidgeted uncomfortably, wondering what thoughts were passing through the mind of this strange and rather frightening person. Richard's first thoughts, that the man might not be entirely sane, came back to him, and he began to feel really frightened.

A man like this might be capable of anything. He didn't want them here and he didn't want to take them away. Then what on earth did he intend to do? It was a question they were afraid to ask themselves.

But in spite of the fears, matters of more immediate

concern occupied their minds: the simple elemental facts of hunger and thirst. Richard screwed up his courage.

"Do you think you could spare us anything to eat or drink?" he asked.

The sheer unexpectedness of the question made the man stare. Then he threw back his head and let out a great laugh.

"Hungry, eh! Then you'd better get yourselves some more coconuts. Come to think of it, I wouldn't mind one myself. It would be a change from the same old diet. Get me a coconut and you can have a slice of bread each. That's all. I have to get my food from the mainland, and I haven't enough to feed all of you."

He led the way along the now familiar beach for a distance of about thirty yards and then stopped abruptly, turning to face them with something of the air of a conjuror about to perform a spectacular trick.

They looked at him questioningly and gazed all about them, but there was nothing to be seen but the empty vista of sea, sand and jungle. He was obviously enjoying the moment.

"All right," he said. "You, little brown monkey, go and get some coconuts. I'll get some bread. Wait here," he said to the others, and turning on his heel, walked into the blank wall of greenness.

9 The jungle hideout

Kitchie had gone off to get more coconuts. Richard turned to Wong.

"What do you make of it?" he asked, speaking in a low voice.

"Not like," Wong said flatly, and his usually cheerful face was troubled.

Richard frowned thoughtfully.

"We'll have to get away," he declared. "He must have a boat somewhere—he makes trips to get food. If we could get hold of it, while he's asleep or something, he couldn't come after us."

Wong nodded, none too happily. He evidently didn't think much of their prospects.

"Not easy," he said. "He watch." He broke off abruptly as the man emerged from the jungle. He was carrying a large loaf, far from fresh, a can of beef, and a bottle, all of which he threw down on the beach.

"All right," he said. "Where's the Malay kid?"

Almost as though he had heard, Kitchie came running along at that moment and threw four coconuts on the ground.

The man took a knife from his belt and hacked off four thick slices from the loaf. Grudgingly he tossed one to each of the boys. They accepted it hungrily. It was, after all, the first food they had had, other than coconuts, since yesterday.

They broke open the coconuts and ate some of the nut with the bread. The man, meanwhile, had opened the can of corned beef and cut himself a good slice, but he didn't offer any to the boys. He also opened the bottle and took a swig from it, smacking his lips with satisfaction.

He sat back watching them with a thoughtful frown.

"What the devil am I to do with you?" he muttered.

"Couldn't you take us with you the next time you go for provisions?" Richard suggested. "You could drop us somewhere and we could find our own way home."

"And come back with the pol—with a lot of other people!"

"Why don't you want anybody to know you're here?" Richard asked daringly.

"Mind your own business! I told you before, you ask too many questions. One thing's certain: somehow or other, I've got to get rid of you!"

There was silence. It was brought home to the boys forcibly that their position was becoming dangerous and unless they were discovered, or somehow managed to make their escape, something really serious might happen. Whatever this man was, whatever he had done, he didn't intend anyone to find him. He must have good cause for hiding.

Already Richard was toying with desperate ideas of escape. Would it be possible for the three of them to overpower this man and tie him down while they made off in his canoe? But the man looked strong, and Richard doubted whether he and his two companions could cope with him. Could they steal off while he was asleep? Could they contrive some sort of signal which would be seen at a distance and bring someone to the rescue? Certainly they must try to do something. It was no use just sitting back and waiting for a rescue that might never come.

Richard's eyes wandered to the point in the wall of jungle where the bearded man had gone to get the food. He would have liked to go in there; it was there, evidently, that this man had some sort of hideout, and it was almost certainly in there that the boat was hidden. How else could he have come here except by boat?

They had finished their rough meal and the man was taking a final swig from the bottle.

"Better than water," he grunted, licking his lips.

Suddenly he froze, staring out across the shining

waters. The boys followed the direction of his gaze and saw something that made their hearts jump.

A boat was approaching the island; a trim white motorboat, skimming along, pushing up great waves on either side of her bows and leaving a broad wake like a white path across the shining silver of the sea.

With a muttered oath the man jumped to his feet.

"Get in there!" he commanded. He grabbed Kitchie and Wong, who happened to be nearest, and bundled them toward the jungle.

"You, too!" he said to Richard.

Richard hesitated for the fraction of a second, but the scowl on the man's face warned him that this was no time to take chances, and he reluctantly followed the other two. Well, he had wanted to see the hideout. Maybe now he might learn something that would help him to think out a more sensible plan of escape.

The man had parted the foliage and once more they ventured into the dim green underworld of the jungle.

An extraordinary sight met their eyes.

Bush and trees had been cut back to form a large clearing about twenty feet square. It had been lined with boxes, bits of driftwood and plantain leaves to form a rough sort of room. An upturned box served as a table, and in one corner some rugs had been arranged to form a bed. There were tools, a saw, a Malay parang, a hurricane lamp, boxes of canned food and a cask. But the object that caught and held Richard's eye was a canoe. It lay in the front of the clearing, barely concealed by the drooping greenery; a spacious twelve-foot craft, light and easily manageable, ready to be pushed through the soft sand to the edge of the water. It would be so easy. . . .

Richard became aware of the man's penetrating eyes boring into him and hastily shifted his gaze.

They had been bundled unceremoniously into the place, and Richard had seen all this in a single glance.

"Get down," the man said, "and keep quiet or it'll be the worse for you."

He wasn't going to take any chances. Picking up a piece of rope, he tied Richard's hands and feet.

"That'll take care of you," he growled. "And just to be sure you don't yell . . ." He picked up a piece of rag which he bound roughly across the boy's mouth. Richard wriggled protestingly but there was nothing he could do. The man was strong and in no mood to be trifled with.

Kitchie and Wong had watched this with wide eyes, too frightened to utter a sound, realizing only too well that it would be their turn next.

In a matter of minutes all three were securely bound and gagged. Their captor glared at them, then crawled cautiously to the edge of the clearing and peered out.

Straining their ears, the boys could hear the sound of the boat engine coming closer. They could see that the man was tense.

Their hopes began to rise, but with hope came an ac- companying fear. This man was obviously desperate and it was clearly of the greatest importance to him that he shouldn't be found. He must have been on this place for some time; he had gone to a great deal of trouble to make himself a home where he couldn't be seen, and had laid in provisions for a long stay. Why? Had he committed some crime and was hiding from the police? And if he had committed one crime that had forced him into hiding, would he hesitate to commit another to escape detection?

These thoughts passed through their minds as the boat approached, leaving them in doubt whether to welcome the approach of a probable rescue.

For minutes that seemed like hours they waited and wondered. What would happen if the boat landed? Would its occupants find the hiding place? And if they did, then what? It was frightening to think what this man might do.

The steady chug-chug of the engine seemed to remain the same for a long time; it no longer appeared to be drawing nearer, nor was it receding. The fact was, although the boys didn't know, that the boat had turned and was following a course parallel with the coast. This was evident a few minutes later when the sound of the engines began to grow fainter.

Their immediate feeling was one of relief, to be followed by one of dismay. This was perhaps their only chance of rescue, and it had gone.

The man was grinning broadly as he turned around.

"So much for that," he said, with great satisfaction.

"Now you can see how things stand. Nobody thinks there's anybody on this island." He surveyed them for a few moments with amusement, then one by one he removed the gags and began to untie them.

"Well then," Richard said, as the gag was removed, "what are you going to do with us?"

The blue eyes gave him a cold, unfriendly glare.

"Yes," he said, "what *am* I going to do with you? I don't know. But understand this: whatever happens to you, it's your own fault. Everything was all right until you came. It would have been all right still, but now . . ."

"What are you worried about?" Richard asked.

The man didn't answer. His gaze had gone to a small suitcase which stood in the corner of the clearing. He regarded it for a moment with a strange look in his eyes, and then with an effort shifted his gaze.

"Maybe," he said softly, "it's time I moved on. It doesn't matter what happens to you. I'll just leave you here. You can go on living on coconuts. By the time they find you—if they ever do—I'll be miles away."

Richard looked quickly at his two companions and saw the fright in their eyes.

"You wouldn't do that! We might . . ."

"Oh, wouldn't I? You'll see about that. Tomorrow. Yes, tomorrow. I'll pack the boat and you can stay here all by yourselves. You can even have my house! I took a lot of trouble over this—but I never thought it was for three kids!"

He stood up and looked around, taking stock of his possessions and noting the things he would need to take: food, tools. His eyes went again to the suitcase. He allowed his hands to linger over it lovingly.

It dawned on Richard then that this case held the answer to a great many questions. If they could get hold of it and discover what was inside, it might explain everything and answer their own problem.

It could only be done if the man was asleep. They must watch and wait for a chance.

10 *Escape!*

Their chance came much sooner than they could have dared to hope. The events of the morning had been unnerving, not only for them but for their captor; moreover the sun was blazing out of a cloudless sky. The combination of heat and exhaustion prompted the man to open another bottle of liquor. He made himself comfortable on his couch and began to drink, pausing between gulps to cast baleful glances at the boys, with an occasional muttered threat thrown in.

Before long he began to drowse. He emptied the bottle, settled himself comfortably and was soon snoring gently.

The boys sat quietly watching and hoping, not daring to move or speak. The snores grew louder and soon the man was in a deep sleep.

They waited a little longer. Then, with fast-beating

heart, Richard got up and began to move around, the others watching him with eyes wide with alarm. He didn't go right to the case, but moved around, noting with a certain admiration the cleverness with which the hideaway had been constructed. The place had clearly been designed for a long stay, and Richard judged that it had already been occupied for a long time.

He paused from time to time to cast a glance at the sleeping man, but he was still in a deep sleep and looked as if he would stay that way.

Screwing up his courage, Richard reached for the case. With bated breath he lifted it. It was heavy. He put it down quickly and tried the catch. It wasn't locked.

Gently he raised the lid, and opened his eyes wide. The other two craned forward to see.

The case was stuffed with bank notes: Straits dollars, the currency of the country. None of them had ever seen so much money in their lives. There must have been thousands of dollars.

So that was the answer. The man was a thief, and no small thief either: a bank robber maybe. Richard stifled an exclamation and quickly closed the case. He lifted it again to replace it, but the clasp hadn't caught properly. The lid fell open and the notes fell to the ground.

There was a moment of petrified silence. Then with shaking hands, Richard began to stuff the notes back into the case. The others helped.

The man stirred, blinked, and opened his eyes. The three boys froze with horror. For a second the man blinked dazedly, then understanding dawned.

"You little fiends!" he shouted, suddenly wide awake.

He leaped to his feet and swung a savage blow at Richard. It caught him on the side of the head and sent him reeling into a corner. Almost in the same instant the man aimed a vicious kick at Wong, who just managed to avoid the full force of it. Kitchie, who was the farthest away, took to his heels and ran as though pursued by devils.

The man picked up the case and began to shove the notes back into it.

"You've done it now! Nosy little devils. I'll kill you for this."

He was shaking with fury, and the two boys cowered in alarm, but luckily the man was too busy putting back the money to vent his wrath on them again.

Meanwhile Kitchie ran on through the soft sand. He had no thought but to put as much distance as he could between himself and this furious man.

He stumbled on, his breath coming in gasps, until he rounded a bend and came to the rock where they had spent the previous night. Exhausted, he flung himself into the hollow they had made, and lay, shaken and panting, to recover.

He thought of Richard and Wong, and wondered what was happening to them. He realized, a little guiltily, that his behavior hadn't been very heroic, but he consoled himself with the thought that he could have done nothing to help if he had stayed. It would only have meant that three of them would have been beaten instead of two. Whereas . . .

A thought flashed into his mind. He had been staring in front of him without seeing; now he realized that he was looking straight at the canoe which they had overturned to form a shelter against the wind.

The canoe!

It had leaked under the weight of three boys; but with the weight of only one boy, especially if that one were skilled in the handling of canoes and knew how to adjust his weight so that the weak part was clear of the water, it might reach home. If he could get back, he could bring help.

Agog with excitement, Kitchie jumped to his feet and began to haul the canoe clear of the sand. He cast anxious looks around to make sure that he hadn't been pursued, but there was no sign of anyone. The hideout was on the other side of the island, and it wasn't likely that the man would have left the other two and come this far in search of him.

He righted the canoe, made a swift examination of the patch, which was still intact, and began to slide the canoe down to the water. The paddle still lay on the sand. He picked it up and threw it into the canoe.

A final push and the canoe glided into the water. She floated well. Kitchie waded in and clambered aboard, taking great care to keep his weight on the side opposite the patch. Fortunately the patch was toward the bow, and the weight of one person in the stern without any counterbalancing weight forward raised the bow out of the water. He saw with great satisfaction that it would be possible to paddle for several miles without shipping any water.

With vigor and skill born of long experience, he plied the paddle and the canoe leaped forward. The sea was calm and still, like a sheet of glass under the blazing sun. He was filled with a feeling of elation as the island fell behind. He was safe, and soon he would bring help to his companions and rescue them from this dangerous man.

Back at the hideout matters had come to a head. The man, having put all the money back into the suitcase, was now loading the canoe with all he needed for his voyage to wherever was to be his next stopping place. Food and cans had been flung into the canoe, and of course the case and its precious contents.

Richard and Wong huddled silently in the corner. There was nothing for them to do but keep out of the way, hoping that the man would take no further notice of them. Richard was still dazed from the blow he had received, and his head was buzzing.

"I must get out of here fast," the man was muttering. "Maybe it was time I moved anyhow. And leave you here to rot!"

He picked up his blankets and threw them into the canoe. He took a last look around to make sure there was nothing more he needed and started to push the canoe. It was heavy and he gave a grunt.

"Here! Come on, you two, help me with this—and no funny business or you'll be sorry for it!"

They obeyed meekly and the three of them began to push the craft down to the sea. It was heavy going, for the canoe was well laden, but at last they reached the edge of the water. The man was about to shove her out when he remembered something.

"The water!"

He turned to go back for the cask of water.

Either he hadn't realized the danger or else he thought the boys were too frightened to take advantage of the situation. He was wrong. Richard, fully aware of the danger they were in, was prepared to grasp at any chance, however desperate, to make an escape.

"Quick," he said, shoving Wong into the canoe. "Grab a paddle, we can get a start on him and he'll never catch us."

He gave the canoe a shove and leaped in as she floated clear.

"But what about Kitchie . . . ?" Wong protested.

"We'll come for him—he must be hiding somewhere. Quick, get a move on."

Wong's usually narrow eyes were wide with fear, but he obediently picked up the second paddle. The two paddles swept the water and the canoe, laden as she was, leaped forward. Almost in the same instant the man came from his hideout. He stood for a moment as though rooted to the spot, unable to believe his own eyes. Then he bellowed with rage. He dropped the water cask and came running down the beach.

The two boys, paddling frantically, were about fifteen yards out from the shore when he reached the water and hurled himself in with a great splash.

Wong groaned with fear, but the two plied their paddles with a new frenzy. If he caught them now they would pay dearly for their escapade. There was no knowing what he would do in his rage.

He came swimming toward them with great powerful strokes. Richard and Wong strained at their paddles, but he was gaining on them. However, they were getting farther from the shore, and he couldn't go out too far; nor could he continue swimming at that rate for long, whereas the boys could continue paddling at their speed for an hour or more. He must catch them quickly or not at all.

The distance between swimmer and canoe was diminishing alarmingly. Despite the two boys' efforts he was still gaining. He made a supreme effort and a great fist swept out of the water and came down on the gunwale of the canoe, making it sway and veer around. Quick as a flash, Richard swung his paddle and brought it down on the hand with all the force he could muster. With a howl of pain the man let go.

Some miles away, in a different direction, Kitchie had been paddling doggedly. His arms were beginning to ache and he was cramped from the uncomfortable position he was forced to take, but the canoe was still sailing well and hadn't shipped even a drop of water.

His eyes scanned the great empty expanse of shining

sea. There wasn't a thing in sight, not a boat or a ship, nor a sign of land.

But he must keep on. The lives of his two companions depended on him.

11 *Police to the rescue*

A trim white police launch was speeding out across the sea, one of three which had been engaged in a search for the missing boys since yesterday. It carried a Malay crew of two, a young English police officer and two native policemen.

From time to time the young officer raised a pair of binoculars to his eyes and swept the empty sea, but there was nothing to be seen except an occasional Chinese junk with a great square sail and eyes painted on each side of her ungainly square bows, or a passing liner which set up waves that sent the smaller boat rocking.

The officer was getting a little weary of this unexciting search and wished himself on some more interesting job.

The *serang*, the Malay captain of the boat, squatted on the engine-room hatch and steered with a small brass

wheel. He was a wizened little man with a face like a weather-beaten monkey.

Suddenly he gave an exclamation and pointed a bony brown finger to where a tiny speck showed dark against the glittering silver of the sea. The officer raised his glasses and focused them on the speck, which leaped nearer and took the shape of a canoe.

"Right," he said. "Alter course. I don't suppose it's anything, but we'd better have a look."

The serang spun the wheel deftly and the boat swung around to head toward the canoe.

Watching through his glasses, the officer saw the occupant of the canoe standing up and waving frantically.

"He's seen us," he announced. "He's trying to attract our attention. Give him a couple of blasts on the whistle."

To Kitchie the sound was the sweetest music he had ever heard.

In a short time the launch was alongside, and he was clambering aboard helped by welcoming hands.

Rapidly, breathlessly, he told his story in a jumble of Malay and pidgin English, which the serang translated when necesary for the benefit of the police officer.

"And you must come quickly," Kitchie concluded urgently, "for this man is a bad man and my friends are in great danger."

But the launch had already changed course again and was heading in the direction which Kitchie had pointed out.

The island was already in sight. The launch was fast and went bouncing over the water, seeming at times almost to take flight.

As they drew near, the officer looked through his binoculars again, but there was nothing to be seen but an empty beach and a rock that had the face of a gargoyle.

"You must go around," Kitchie shouted. "It is on the other side that the man lives."

Once again the serang spun the little brass wheel and the boat turned to follow the line of the coast.

As they came around the corner a strange sight met their eyes: a large, well-laden canoe was being paddled furiously out from the shore and a man was swimming after it. The men in the police launch saw the two boys plying their paddles with desperate energy, but neither of the boys was expert in the art of canoeing, and Kitchie's skill and experience were sadly missed. The craft zigzagged uncertainly, and their pursuer was steadily gaining on them. He was a strong swimmer, his course was straight and his rage had given him extra power.

Neither the boys nor the man in the sea had noticed the police launch, which had now rounded the bend and was bearing down on the scene at great speed, throwing out curling waves from her sharply tapered bow.

The swimmer was close to the canoe now. With a tremendous effort he seemed to throw himself half out of the water. His arm swept over and his great fist came down on the gunwale of the canoe, making it stop abruptly and rock so violently that the two boys were nearly thrown overboard.

As the launch sped toward the canoe, the policemen on board saw Richard lift his paddle and bring it down on the man's hand with all the force he could muster.

They heard the man's howl of mingled rage and pain as he released his hold and the canoe steadied itself.

The next moment the police launch was alongside.

The exhausted man was hauled aboard the launch, where he was promptly seized by two Malay constables.

Richard and Wong could only stare unbelievingly. They were still dazed and not at all sure what had happened. Then they saw the brown face of the missing Kitchie grinning at them from the police boat and were more astonished than ever.

Willing hands reached out to help them aboard the launch. The canoe was taken in tow and the suitcase collected. The three boys found themselves at last heading for home.

12 Homecoming

All their parents were waiting on the quayside, for a radio message had been sent to tell them of the boys' rescue. Each was welcomed with relief and joy, to be followed by explanations and lectures.

Bit by bit the story was pieced together. Richard and Wong heard how Kitchie had made his own escape to bring the police to their aid. Kitchie, in turn, had to hear their story. Then came interviews with the police during which they learned more about their captor and, finally, a return trip to the island with a police officer who wanted to see the jungle hideout.

"I suppose you realize," Richard's father had said in the course of his lecture, "that besides giving your mother and me a lot of worry, you've caused a great deal of trouble to a lot of other people. The police have been searching for you day and night."

"I'm sorry, Father," Richard said. "We didn't mean to. It was just the way things turned out."

The young police officer who interviewed each of the boys in turn treated the matter more lightly. He seemed not only to have been in complete sympathy with the spirit of the adventure but was clearly a little envious and rather inclined to wish that he had been a few years younger so that he might even have taken a part in it himself. He was most appreciative, too, of the part the boys had played in the capture of the thief, and Richard found himself warming to the officer and telling his story with a wealth of detail.

"You know," the officer said, "if you hadn't stumbled on him, he'd probably have got clean away."

"He was just lying low till things cooled down a bit, I guess," Richard said. "I got the idea he'd been there for some time."

"Over a month."

"He'd stolen a lot of money, hadn't he?"

"Yes, from some rich Chinese merchants. He was working for them and they trusted him absolutely. It's a bad business when Europeans behave like that. Fortunately, it doesn't often happen. Anyway, you'll read the whole story in the papers."

They heard nothing more for several days. Then one day a police car pulled up in front of Richard's house and his police officer friend stepped out.

"Well," he said with a broad grin. "It's all settled.

You'll read all about it in the papers tomorrow, but there's something you may as well hear from me first. The fact is, the Chinese are always grateful for any little service that is done for them, and they want to show their gratitude to you boys in a practical sort of way."

"You mean," Richard drew a sharp breath, "they want to give us a reward?"

"That's just it!"

Richard's face clouded. His father had what seemed to him rather curious ideas about anything of that sort. He probably would have very strong objections to his son's accepting a monetary reward. Come to think of it, Richard wasn't altogether sure that he approved of the idea himself. It was all very well in a way, but somehow the idea of accepting money for what he and his friends had done just didn't seem the thing to do.

"Well, it's very nice of them, but I don't think it's going to work. You see, I'll have to tell Father . . ."

The police officer smiled.

"Your father knows all about it."

Richard stared in utter astonishment.

"He knows, and he hasn't . . ."

"He wouldn't hear of your accepting money. But there was something which it seemed to everybody was a much better idea and more acceptable to all of you. If you'll come with me in the car . . ."

Feeling completely dazed, Richard followed the police officer into the car and a few moments later they were whirling along the hot dusty road to the beach.

Still wondering, Richard got out and looked around him.

A small crowd had gathered, and in the middle he saw his mother and father—his mother smiling a little, his father detached as ever. And there were Kitchie and Wong, Kitchie's parents, whom he knew, and Wong's parents, whom he had seen once or twice before, and several other people, European, Malays, Chinese—and one rather important-looking Chinese.

Kitchie and Wong were grinning widely. Richard wanted to go over and join them, but should he speak to his parents first?

The police officer decided this question for him by taking him by the arm and leading him over to where the important-looking Chinese was standing.

"I want you to meet Mr. Tan Tok Saik," he said.

The Chinese gentleman bowed gravely. Richard, a little confused, managed a bow of sorts and blushed to the roots of his hair.

Then began a speech conveying the gratitude of Mr. Tan Tok Saik and his associates, enlarging on the great courage of the three boys, and of the desire of all those whose money had been recovered to show their appreciation in some small, unworthy manner.

At this point Richard lost interest in the speech; his eyes had wandered, as though drawn by some invisible power, to the waterline.

There, drawn up on the beach, were three new and shining canoes.

There was no need to hear the rest of what Mr. Tan Tok Saik had to say. It was all quite clear now. The gift, the perfect gift to the people who didn't want to take money, was here. This was the realization of those dreams which had seemed so unattainable only a short time ago. . . .

As in a trance Richard heard the quaint singsong of the Chinese benefactor's voice continuing his speech. Somehow he blurted out his thanks, and then the three of them, Kitchie, Wong and Richard, were down at the beach gazing at those new and lovely things that were their own.

The sun glinted on the wet paddles; the three canoes leaped forward across the sparkling silver of the sunlit sea, out toward the little green islands. The Malay boy, the Chinese boy, and the English boy looked at each other from across the intervening stretches of water that separated the canoes and then grinned. This was joy, this was happiness, this was the supreme understanding.

And from the shore the kindly Mr. Tan Tok Saik watched with a smile that seemed to hold the wisdom of centuries.

"It was truly a wise gift," he said. "For we have given them something far more precious than money."